T0365174

World of Color

Unity through Colors

Copyright © 2004 by Roderick B. Parker. 556269

All rights reserved. No part of this book may be reproduced
or transmitted in any form or by any means, electronic or
mechanical, including photocopying, recording, or by any
information storage and retrieval system, without permission in
writing from the copyright owner.

This is a work of fiction. Names, characters, places and
incidents either are the product of the author's imagination or
are used fictitiously, and any resemblance to any actual persons,
living or dead, events, or locales is entirely coincidental.

To order additional copies of this book, contact:
Xlibris
844-714-8691
www.Xlibris.com
Orders@Xlibris.com

ISBN: Softcover   978-1-6641-4453-8
        Hardcover   978-1-4134-6513-6
        EBook   978-1-4771-7435-7

Library of Congress Control Number: 2003097763

Print information available on the last page

Rev. date: 11/23/2020

World of Color

Reality Check
Unity through Colors

Written By: Roderick B. Parker
Illustrated By: Roderick B. Parker, Terence C. Ball
Edited by: L. Parker

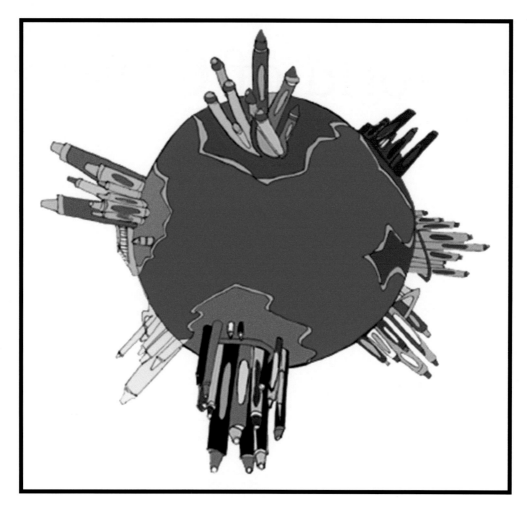

In the beginning of time in crayon world, long, long ago, some used crayons were old and small and others were new and tall. However, there was a big problem in crayon land: they were so divided that each color would not harmonize with another color.

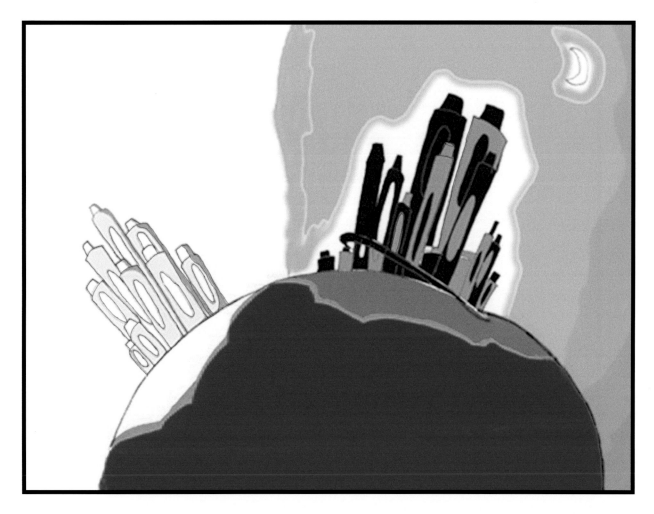

The white crayons were the bosses, pushing white paper with white pads. They lived in white houses, with white cats and white crayons to match.
The black crayons only played with other black crayons, which wore black hats, black heels, and rolled black wheels.

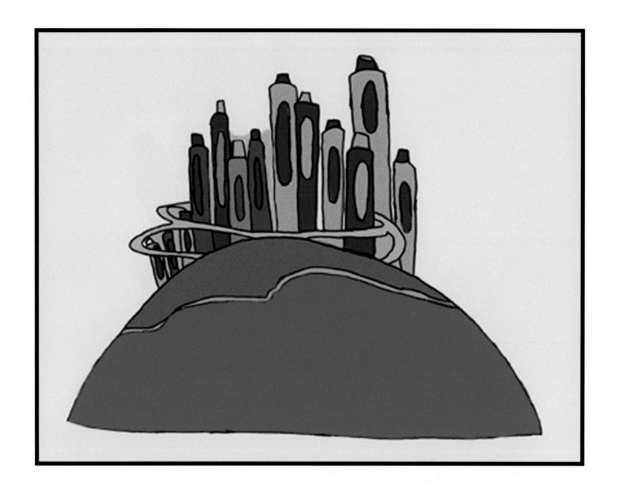

The brown crayons had their own brown town. In it were brown schools, brown houses, brown shoes, and brown mountains with brown trees that had brown leaves. Everywhere you looked, you would see different shades of brown things.

The red crayons had their own red states, with red mates, and red lights so bright that they looked like firebombs at night.

Even the gold crayons had their own homeland. The gold land was sparkling; the sand and the roads were gold. There were gold cars, and tall gold night-lights that were sparkling and shining bright.

The pink crayon land had pink pigs, pink hats, pink mats, and pink bikes with pink lights. Everywhere you looked everything was pink.

In yellow town where only yellow crayons lived, they loved the yellow sun that shined so bright. There were many yellow cabs and yellow houses with yellow flowers along side the yellow-lined streets. There were yellow trees with yellow leaves and many yellow bees.

All of the other colors were just as separated as could be.

The green and purple crayons did not get along. They always fussed and fought because they didn't match. Many of the other colors agreed with that natural fact.

When black crayons were stopped in other colors' land, they would say, "Hold on and step back and let's think about one fact. Black was the first color to outline designs, through time black dittoed the most, and now Xeroxes the most. In fact, all you colors mixed into one make me what I am, that is why I am as black as I am. So can we just get along?"

The other colors responded by saying, "Ok, all of that's alright, but you have to go back to where you came from at night."

There was a crayon man that loved all crayons from every land. Mr. Psychedelic was his name and bringing crayons together was his plan. He told all crayons that they should mix and match, but some of the crayons didn't want to hear any of that. They told Mr. Psychedelic to go back to wherever he came from, talking like that.

    The crayons were laid off last spring because of a new machine, the Bubble Ink Jet Printer 2000-Q.

    So now, what were the crayons to do? How about becoming freelance artists? Is that a surprise to you? Well if you were a crayon, what would you do?

In the beginning of time there were only the primary colors: red, yellow and blue. After some time had passed, some crayons mixed and matched: there was a blue crayon man and a yellow crayon lady with a green crayon baby.

The other crayons did not like it when they saw a red crayon man and a blue crayon lady with a purple crayon baby. To most of them it was so bad, the secondary colors were called out-cast. As a matter of fact, to some they were even called misfits. They could not go into any town and have fun because they were part of multi-colored families.

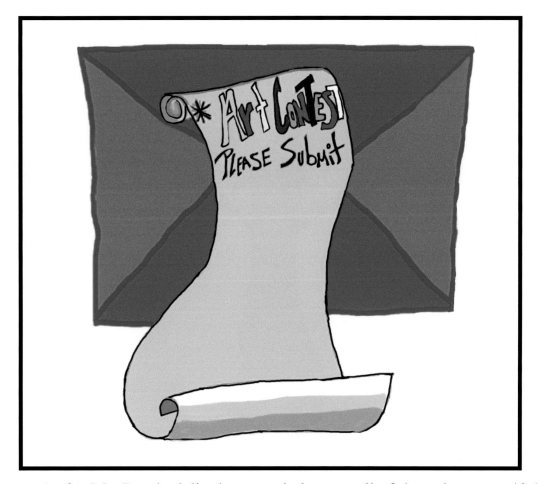

As for Mr. Psychedelic, he was glad to see all of the colors even if they did not match. He had a plan on how to get the crayons to come together; he called his plan, "Millennium Art Project Love Sweep #1." In his mind all colors should mix and match, even though some of those crayons didn't want to do any of that.

So Mr. Psychedelic sent letters to all colors that read like this:

"Art contest—please submit one art piece from each color's land. Send in your entry as soon as you can. We are going to find out who is the best crayon color of the land."

The eighth of December was the due date for the art projects to be delivered to Mr. Psychedelic's place.

When all the art pieces were side by side, Mr. Psychedelic said to himself: "All of these art pieces look the same, the only difference in the artwork are the colors and the names."

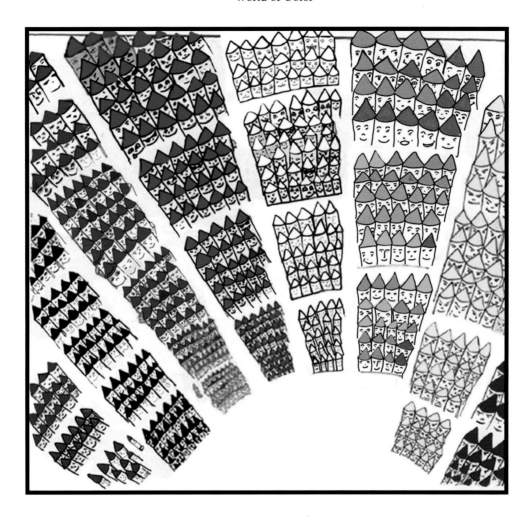

    Mr. Psychedelic called for an art conference to be set for December Twelfth, to give all of the colors the opportunity to judge for themselves.

    On that day, crayons packed the arena like sardines. The green crayons were with the greens, the yellow crayons were with the yellows, the blue crayons were with the blues, the red crayons were with the reds, and the black crayons were with the blacks. All of the colors were still apart and this bothered Mr. Psychedelic's heart.

Mr. Psychedelic stepped on to the stage and shouted, "This is going to be a historic day! We're going to find out who's the best crayon color of us all!"

He turned on the sound meter as he held the first picture over his head. No doubt about it, this picture was red—only that section screamed out of its head. The red crayons started jumping and clapping as they pumped up the sound meter which read 16%. The other color sections began shaking their heads, saying the artwork looked good but the color was bad.

Color after color, art after art, the sound meter read the same, 16%. As you can tell, all of the colors only voted for themselves.

Just then the multi-colored families came through the door, they mixed and matched way in the back. Mr. Psychedelic smiled and said, "Yes! I like that."

Mr. Psychedelic announced that the art contest was a tie, and said, "It's really bad and sad to think that no color likes any other color other except its own." He asked for a brown crayon representative to come up on stage to do its art thing.

Now the brown representative was smart, it started drawing at the top of the wall on stage, first going high and then low. The brown section jumped to the floor, clapping, cheering, and asking for more!

Mr. Psychedelic told brown to sit down and asked for a blue representative to come up on stage. But the blue crayons were mad and sad and all in a huff, stating, "We don't get along with brown, we don't match and that's a fact! We aren't going to do any of that!"

Mr. Psychedelic shook his head and said, "If you don't send a representative up to do your blue color on this wall, your section will be disqualified and we will never see who is the best crayon of us all."

So a blue representative hurried and got busy doing its art thing. When it finished the blue and brown section began dancing around, giving each other high-fives and handshakes.

The other sections began mumbling to themselves saying, "The art looked good but the colors were bad" until their color crayon stepped on stage, then their section acted as if it was a parade: they were jumping, clapping, and singing songs! Before too long, all the sections were dancing all over the place.

With one color section left, the black crayon sent a representative to outline the art. There was so much shouting that the noise meter broke! No one could hear what was coming out of Psychedelic's throat.

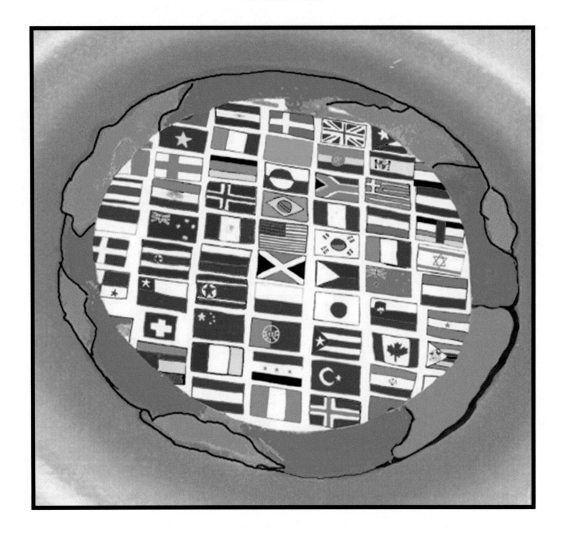

    When black was finished, there were "oohs" and "ahhs", and then there was silence. Suddenly all the crayons went wild clapping and cheering good cheers!

    Mr. Psychedelic turned but was too close to see, so he backed up and the art piece came in clear view for him to see. He saw a rainbow with all of the colors in it: In the middle of the rainbow was a circle, which resembled the world, and in the center of the circle were all the flags from around the world.

Mr. Psychedelic smiled and raised his hand, putting his thumb straight up over his head and said, "Everyone wins!" Mr. Psychedelic called for all the crayon representatives to come up on stage. "Come on up, white! Come on up black, brown, yellow, gold, pink and red!" Once all the colors were united on stage, Mr. Psychedelic told all of the colors to bow and throw a kiss to celebrate what they had made.

All of the cameras clicked and flashed, and after this event had passed, all the colors mixed and matched together in the crayon box, making beautiful art works together around the world.